# Not Yet, Nathan!

Sue Perry and Jane Rose

Illustrated by Jan Lewis

**CAMBRIDGE**
UNIVERSITY PRESS

Hello! I'm Nathan.

Here is my family.
We live in a trailer.

One day I wanted to go swimming, but
we had to go shopping instead.

It took such a long time that I was getting thirsty.

"Can I have a drink, Mum?" I said.

"Not yet, Nathan," said Mum.

"Can I have a drink now, Dad?" I said.

"No, not yet, Nathan," said Dad.

The lorry went up and down.
My drink went up and down.

"Can I have a drink *now*, Mum?" I said.

"No, not yet, Nathan," said Mum.

At last, we arrived home.

"*Please* can I have a drink now?" I said.

"OK, Nathan," everyone said.

I began to open the bottle.

The bottle was hissing and . . .

"Not yet, Nathan!" everyone shouted.